Happy
Chan____.
w/ Big love +
Affection

THE ADVENTURES OF

Mrs. Jesus

♡
M, S; R

THE ADVENTURES OF

Mrs.

WILLIAM MORROW
An Imprint of HarperCollins Publishers

Jesus

DAN O'SHANNON

HarperCollins books may be purchased for educational, business, or sales promotional use. For information please e-mail the Special Markets Department at SPsales@harpercollins.com.

FIRST EDITION

Library of Congress Cataloging-in-Publication Data has been applied for.

ISBN 978-0-06-234061-0

14   15   16   17   18   ID6/RRD   10 9 8 7 6 5 4 3 2 1

for my mother

6

seriously, i want to know about those footprints in the sand. there were two sets, except when things got hard for us, then there was only one. what's the deal?

does this have anything to do with that mary magdalene?

I plead the fifth.

19

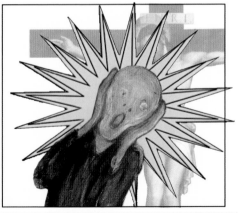

the adventures of *mrs. jesus*

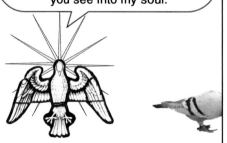

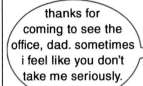

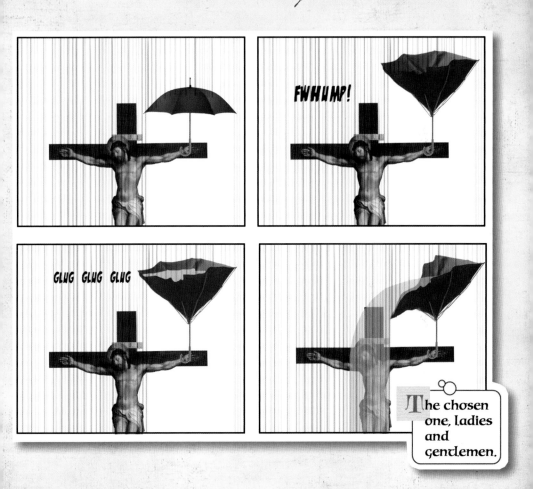

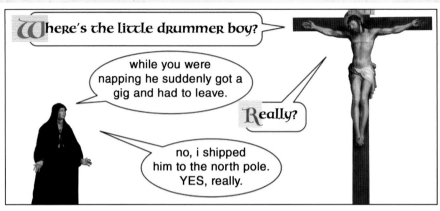

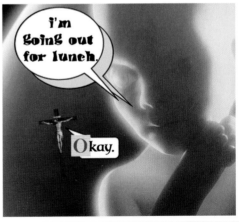

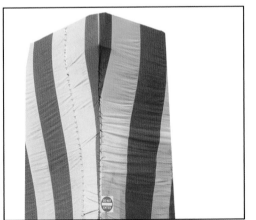

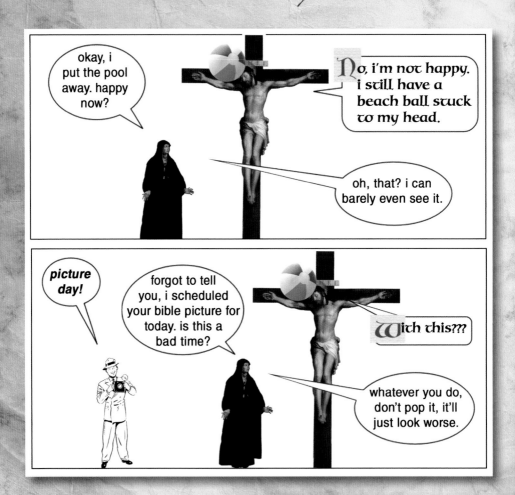

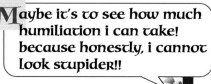

the adventures of *mrs. jesus*

86

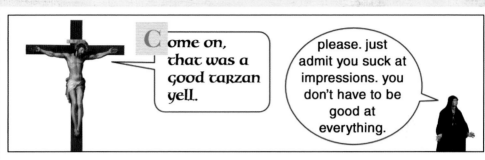

the adventures of *mrs. jesus*

94

the adventures of *mrs. jesus*

99

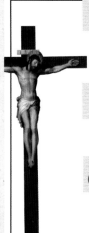

If we build crosses, aren't we to blame for all deaths by crucifixion?

we just make them. we're not responsible for what a few lunatics do with them.

But they can't crucify if we stop selling them.

they'll just find some other way to kill, or get crucifixes from other countries.

What if we just make it harder for people to get them?

if everyone has a cross to bear, we all have a right to bear crosses. you can't take away our rights.

It's a tough one.

don't worry. one day, crucifixion will go out of style and we won't even have this argument anymore.

the adventures of *mrs. jesus*

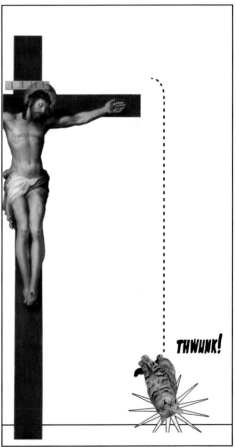

No!

>   why not?

Because it's a stupid idea!

>   i could put it on the bulletin board!
>   please? it only costs a dollar!

That's not the point!

>   how come we only do things
>   you want and never anything
>   i want?

Fine.

>   was that so hard? i promise,
>   you won't be sorry.

excuse me, ma'am. my crew and i are putting up this billboard for the new movie *a heist too far.* mind if we lean some of the pieces against your husband's cross while we go on break?

i can't see any problem with that.

wild guess: you managed to find a problem.

132

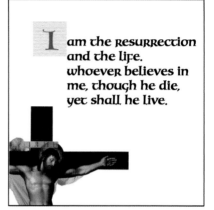

the adventures of *mrs. jesus*

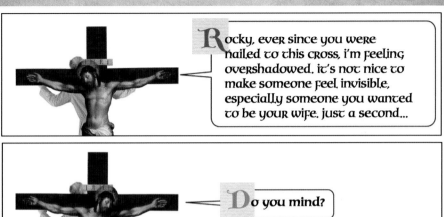

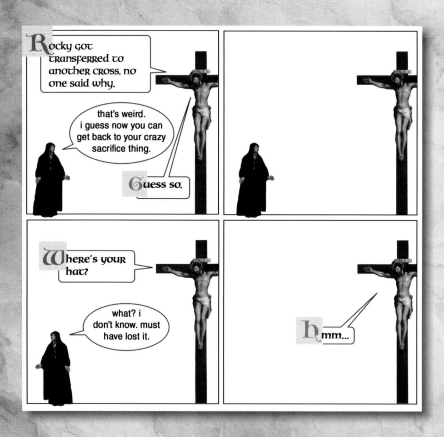

This is the part where I acknowledge everyone, and I have to start by thanking Mrs. Jesus.

Two years ago, for reasons that are unimportant now, I was mired in a long bout of crippling depression and anxiety. During this period, I doodled the first Mrs. Jesus cartoon on a script at work. I don't know where the idea came from, it was just popped into my head. (This was before a spate of news articles about a possible wife for Jesus made the rounds.) A couple nights later, I thought I'd post it on Facebook. Rather than redraw it, however, I used images from an old painting (*Crucifixion With the Virgin, Mary Magdalene and St. John the Evangelist,* by Nicolò Dell' Abate), repurposing

Mary Magdalene as the fictional Mrs. Jesus. I barely
remember doing it, but I remember the immediate
reaction: a couple people liked it and my mother
unfriended me. Encouraged by these responses,
I did another the next night. And then another. As
time went on, I found myself looking forward to the
nights of quiet work, and the absurd results. I had no
thoughts of a book, or of anything beyond the work
itself. But by giving me this sliver of purpose, Mrs.
Jesus began my return to the world from a black
despair.

Mrs. Jesus saved me.

She started as a standard nagging wife, but I soon
felt empathy for her. After all, how do all-too-human
humans behave when one of their own is raised to
deity status? Self-worth, hubris, denial, projection,

and passive aggression became themes straight from my therapist's office. Oh, and there's that Scream kid. We're still working on that one. Style-wise, the earlier cartoons owe a bit to the comic strip *Red Meat,* by Max Cannon. I love the never-changing expressions and the pauses of wordless panels.

More people to thank:

Everyone at *Modern Family,* particularly Abraham Higginbotham, who kept my original drawing, and Danny Zuker, who appears as a Twitter-obsessed character in a few of the cartoons. Also the eternally optimistic Katie Johnson, who pushed me to get this thing out there, and introduced me to Don Bitters, who made my cobbled pictures into hi-res images. Thanks to Chelsey Emmelhainz, and to the enthusiastic and supportive May Chen at HarperCollins. Also, how about

this layout, huh? Thanks to Lorie Pagnozzi for making
it all come together.

And of course the people on Facebook—too
numerous to mention individually—who faithfully
followed Mrs. J's adventures. (Although I will note
Linda Mathius, who wrote the first positive comment
on the first post.) Many likes to all of you.

the end